Library of Congress Cataloging-in-Publication Data available.
ISBN 978-1-4521-1233-6

Manufactured in China.

Design by Amelia May Mack.
Typeset in Mr Eaves, Mrs Eaves, and Trend.
The illustrations in this book were rendered in ink and watercolor.

10 9 8 7 6

Chronicle Books LLC
680 Second Street
San Francisco, California 94107

Chronicle Books—we see things differently. Become part of our
community at www.chroniclekids.com.

HOW TO READ A STORY

By Kate Messner
Illustrated by Mark Siegel

THE PRINCESS THE DRAGON, AND THE ROBOT

chronicle books · san francisco

STEP 1

FIND A STORY.

A good one.
It can have princesses and castles,
if you like that sort of thing,
or witches and trolls.
(As long as they're not too scary.)

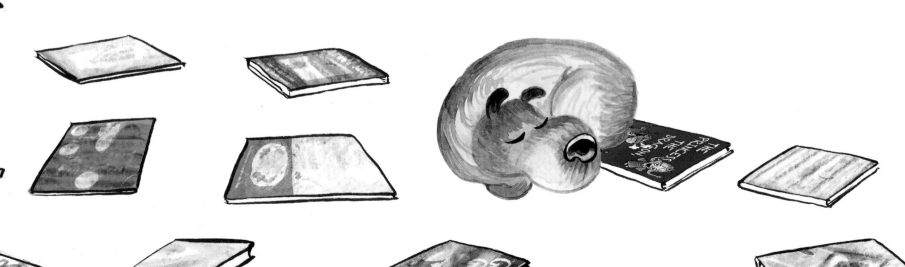

STEP 2

FIND A READING BUDDY.

A good one.

A buddy can be older . . .

or younger . . .

or a person your age.

Or maybe not a person at all.

Make sure your reading buddy is nice and snuggly.
And make sure you both like the book.
If you don't agree . . . go back to Step 1.
Sometimes it takes a few tries to find just the right book.

FIND A COZY READING SPOT.

Outside is fun . . . but not if it's very cold.
Unless you have thick woolen blankets,
and hats and scarves, and cups of steaming
hot cocoa.

And not if it's very hot.
Unless you have trees to shade you from the sun,
a hammock to catch cool breezes, and tall glasses
of icy lemonade.

Inside is good.
Couches are cozy. So are chairs big enough for two.

Just be careful not to get stuck.

STEP 4

LOOK AT THE BOOK'S COVER.

Can you guess what it's about?
Read the title. That might be a clue.

STEP 5

OPEN THE BOOK.

(This is the exciting part!)

"Once
a

Read the story in a loud, clear voice,
not too slow and not too fast.

You can point to words if you like,
but you don't have to do that.

upon

time . . . "

When the characters talk,
whatever's being said . . .
say it in a voice to match who's talking.

"I will save
the kingdom."

"I am the
most POWERFUL
in all the land!"

STEP 7

No matter what you read,
hold the book so your buddy can see the pictures.
Buddies get impatient when they can't see well.

If there are words you don't know,
try sounding them out or looking at the
pictures to see what makes sense.

"They were afraid the dragon would burn down the **cass . . . cass . . . Oh . . .** The **castle!**"

They were afraid the dragon would burn down the castle.

If you need a break, you can pause for a minute . . .
and talk to your reading buddy
to predict what might happen next.

Will the castle catch on fire?
Will the princess tame the dragon?
Will the robot marry the princess?
Will the horse make friends with the dragon?
Will the dragon eat them all for lunch?

When you get to the exciting parts,
make your voice sound exciting, too.

"Who dares disturb me in

my cave?" the dragon growled.

"Oh dear! Oh no!"

The robot was so scared all
his metal parts rattled.
What would they do?

But the princess tackled that
dragon and held him down.

"You must promise you'll
leave our kingdom in peace!"

When you and your buddy can't stand it a second longer . . .

turn the page to read how things work out.

The dragon promised and decided it was better being friends.

And they all lived happily ever after.

STEP 10

When the book is over, say,

"The End."

The dragon promised and decided it was better being friends.

And they all lived happily ever after.

And then . . . if it was a really good story . . .
go right back to the beginning
and start all over again.